KR FEB 2012
OFJan 14
WK APR 2015
KL JUN 2018
KD SEP 2015
KL MAR 2017

# Dogs Don't Eat Jam

## and Other Things Big Kids Know

Story by Sarah Tsiang        Art by Qin Leng

annick press
toronto + new york + vancouver

We acknowledge the support of the Canada Council for the Arts, the Ontario
Arts Council, and the Government of Canada through the Canada Book
Fund (CBF) for our publishing activities.

 ONTARIO ARTS COUNCIL
CONSEIL DES ARTS DE L'ONTARIO


Cataloging in Publication

Tsiang, Sarah
        Dogs don't eat jam and other things big kids know / by Sarah Tsiang ;
illustrated by Qin Leng.


ISBN 978-1-55451-360-4 (bound).—ISBN 978-1-55451-359-8 (pbk.)


        I. Leng, Qin  II. Title.


PS8639.S583D64 2011          jC813'.6          C2011-900984-6


Distributed in Canada by:
Firefly Books Ltd.
66 Leek Crescent
Richmond Hill, ON
L4B 1H1

Published in the U.S.A. by Annick Press (U.S.) Ltd.
Distributed in the U.S.A. by:
Firefly Books (U.S.) Inc.
P.O. Box 1338
Ellicott Station
Buffalo, NY 14205


Printed in China


Visit us at: www.annickpress.com
Visit Sarah Tsiang at: http://sarahtsiang.wordpress.com
Visit Qin Leng at: http://www.qinleng.com

For my big brother, Francis, who taught me how
to burp and make a perfect snowball.
—S.T.

To Lian, for teaching me how to be a great sister.
—Q.L.

# So you've been born!
# Congratulations.

I'm big now, but you know what? I wasn't always this big. As your older sister, I'm here to help. I've put together this handy guide to life.

It took a lot of time and hard work to get to where I am now.

You might look at me and see that I can pull up my zipper,

brush my hair,

and tie my own shoes (mostly).

I can even get up and
feed the dog before Mom
and Dad. I'm very helpful.

But I wasn't always this way.

I was actually born tiny, just like you. But
even when I was little, I had important things
to do. The first thing was to make parents.

Before I was born, they weren't
Mom and Dad. They were Wanda
and Bob. I gave them a promotion.

Before you, I was just me. Now I'm a big sister.
And you're a little brother. So see? You've done
something great already.

Everything is going to be new to you. I was a baby so long ago it's hard to remember, but I guess it's like going to another planet where everyone talks gobbledygook and eats with their ears.

You're learning to drink milk. You'll learn to hold your head up and how to look around.

Right now you can't even tell Mom or Dad that your toe is itchy or that you're too hot. You have to cry when something is wrong.

But you'll learn new
things every day. You'll
learn about broccoli and
cheese and yams.

You'll learn that things fall down

(you'll learn that a lot).

You'll even learn that sounds can come from all sorts of body parts (yep, just like that).

If you learn how to go, it's important to learn how to stop.

You'll find out that you can be loud, louder, and loudest (I'll help you with that).

You'll learn to smile and to laugh, and even how to make other people laugh. I did— and all this was before my first birthday.

If there is one thing a baby wants, it's to become a toddler, which means walking around.

Grown-ups are fast, so you'll want to be faster!

You'll have to practice every day. I pulled myself up on chairs, on the coffee table, and on the dog.

Don't try the dog.

I fell a lot. But I got back up again,
even if I did need a little cry first.

I never gave up and you won't either. People clapped and cheered when I could finally get to the books on the coffee table by myself.

The next thing you'll have to
learn is how to talk. Grown-ups
use millions of words every day.

Take it from me, it's best to learn
the most important ones first.

But don't stop there. You'll want to name everything—

you'll want to name the whole world.

You'll spend hours learning
how much cups can hold.
And how much they can't.

We'll read piles of stories, about monkeys
and toothpaste and everything. Just
remember not to chew on my books.

You'll learn how to brush your own teeth, and that you're allowed to spit in CERTAIN places.

When you get bigger you'll
even get rid of diapers! I did
and I never looked back.

Of course, it won't all be smooth. You might have some trouble with Mom and Dad.

I did when they were in their bossy stage,

always telling me which way to put on my pants,

or where to paint,

or that the dog
doesn't eat jam.

Take it from me. Sometimes you'll get angry with Mom and Dad. But three minutes of quiet time is a lot longer than three minutes of T.V.

You'll learn that mad goes away but love stays.

Hugs can make mad go away even faster.

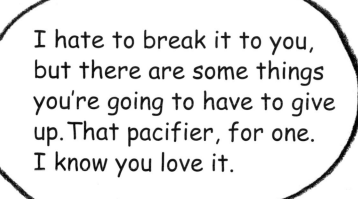

I hate to break it to you, but there are some things you're going to have to give up. That pacifier, for one. I know you love it.

I had one that helped me to sleep too. But that was before I slept in my big bed. It's hard to give up some things, but that's part of being big.

When you're as big as me you'll be able
to do things without Mom and Dad.

I had to leave them by
themselves to go to
kindergarten. They
were very brave.

Now I ride a big
yellow bus

and I'm learning to count
as high as the sky.

I can print my letters (except for K)

and make a puppet out of toilet paper rolls.

And believe it or not, little baby, one day you'll be just as big as I am.

With a little help, of course.